Love & Be

With
Love &
Best Witches
Maria
Mann

Love & Best Witches

Maria Mann

easyBroom

Love & Best Witches

An easyBroom book

Copyright © 2010 Maria Mann

ISBN 978-0-9576288-0-9

The right of Maria Mann to be identified as the author of this work has been asserted in accordance with Sections 77 and 78 of the Copyright, Designs and Patents Act 1988

Illustrations and Cover Design: Maria Mann

All rights reserved

No part of this publication may be reproduced, stored in a retrieval system or transmitted in any form or by any means without the prior written permission of the publisher, nor be otherwise circulated in any form of binding or cover other than that in which it is published and without a similar condition being imposed on the subsequent publisher

A catalogue record of this book is available from The British Library

Maria Mann is the author of the best selling

Verity Red's Diary
A story of surviving M.E.

She has had M.E. for seventeen years and when
she is not working on her books, loves to rest
with her cats or do a healing spell...

for Louise, Dad and Jay

&

In memory of my beloved cats; Paddy, Murphy, Horace and Claudia.

Acknowledgements

Love and gratitude to my partner Nigel for doing all the typing, scanning all my illustrations into the computer, and helping me put the whole book together. Hugs and thanks to Julia and Paul, for their help with the editing and Jess for technical info.

Heartfelt thanks to my dear friends: Jay and Pete for their inspiring comments and brilliant CDs that kept me company during the long hours of drawing; Len, for his lovely poem, Dreams; Sarah, for being Sarah; Jim, for his delightful poems, Christopher Robin Online and Disappointed Snail Fanatic; Sally for her thoughtfulness, and Rachel for the witches' cookbook.

Loving hugs to my beautiful niece Louise, whose letters were the inspiration for this book and the title. Thank you for your fabulous poem; Witch, Witch, and drawings of a dragon and a witch.

Last but not least to my cats. For endless warm furry love, lost pens, inspiration, and marvellous muddy paw prints all over my manuscript.

Prologue

Once upon a time there was a little girl who had a special pen-friend, her auntie Nettie. Auntie wasn't very well because she had an illness called M.E. but she could write lovely letters when her hands didn't ache and she was fun to be with, when well enough for a small visitor, if she hadn't been overdoing it.

Auntie overdid it if she spent too long in the kitchen baking Harry Potter chocolate frog cookies or making magical sparkly lemonade; travelling on her broomstick in cold weather without wearing witchy thermal underwear, or doing spells involving: lots of chanting, anointing, collecting of herbs, picking up of heavy goblets, picking up of heavy goblins, ringing of bells or wand waving.

Chapter One

Auntie Nettie's Birthday

My name is Louise and I like writing to my auntie, she is a witch! Next time I visit her she is going to help me with my witchy spelling, I am very excited!! She has a broomstick which is very old and needs some repairs. It is due for an MOT with the pixie mechanics soon because it has done a lot of mileage. Auntie said she hasn't got the energy to bump-start it anymore either. I told her she should get a broomstick servicing kit like the one Hermione gave Harry for his birthday, in the book, Harry Potter and the Prisoner of Azkaban. The kit contains: A large jar of Fleetwoods high finish handle polish, a pair of gleaming silver tail twig clippers, a tiny brass compass to clip onto your broom for long journeys and a handbook of do-it-yourself broom care.

Auntie has four witchy hats. Two are party-pointy hats, one is a luminous designer hat for special occasions like Halloween, and the other one is plain black for travelling in all weathers.

Instead of wearing black witchy clothes, auntie wears jeans or leggings with tee-shirts or jumpers. She says jeans and tee-shirt are just as appropriate for spell work as ritual robes. When auntie rides on her broomstick she wears old black witchy clothes because people don't expect to see a witch on a broomstick wearing jeans and a tee-shirt.

I've seen auntie's old black clothes on her washing line. I asked her why they were a bit torn and had burn marks. She said she used to fly too low over tree tops and TV aerials. The burn marks were made by small dragons who flew with her once, they were just being friendly. The pixies are sometimes naughty because they like to ride on her hat and steal the odd sequin. They use sequins for money to pay the fairies to make them little jackets and hats. The fairies love sequins because they look pretty when they are sewn onto their party dresses.

At the end of my last letter to auntie I wrote Love and Best Witches. Auntie said it made her

cackle a lot so now she writes Love and Best Witches in her letters and Best Witches on the envelopes. I am going to learn how to cackle.

On Friday I won a prize for being the best witch in the fun run at school. I won a dalmatian pencil case that barks! Auntie is very proud of me and made a certificate. It has very witchy black writing and mum is going to buy a clip-frame so I can hang it on the wall.

Best. Witch

awarded to

Louise

for being the
best dressed witch
in the fun run

Well done!

We are going to make Harry Potter chocolate frog cookies next time I visit auntie. I saw what we will need in her recipe book, The Witch's Kitchen.

The instructions say that if you are a little witch, you should always remember to ask a grown-up to help, particularly when you use a hot oven. Auntie says we will have to manage without a grown-up and make do with a silly old witch!

In her wardrobe I saw a long black velvet cloak with a silvery lining. Mum says, every cloud has a silver lining, I say every cloak has a silver lining!

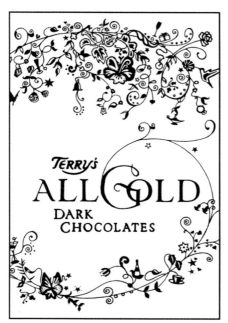

Last Sunday was Auntie Nettie's birthday. She is quite old, forty-nine years old!! She says she feels ancient sometimes. I gave her a birthday card with a picture of a cat because auntie likes cats, especially black ones. I gave her dark chocolates too because she likes them best. They were Terry's All Gold dark chocolates with a fairytale picture on the front. Auntie spent so long looking at it, I thought she had fallen asleep.

Mum said I should have given her Black Magic chocolates but auntie is a good witch (she does not do black magic). She practices green witchcraft and only does healing spells using herbs, candles and oils. Auntie chants a lot of weird words too, which I don't understand, but I am going to learn them.

Auntie's witchy friends made her birthday cards. They used black card, pressed herbs, stick on bats and frogs, and glitter from Hobby Witch Craft. They like to shop there because there are special parking spaces for broomsticks. People who ride motor-bikes and bicycles are afraid to use the parking spaces because they get their wheels clamped by the pixie police. The pixies use very strong magical bindweed to clamp the wheels.

If your wheels get clamped you have to visit a witch to say sorry. You can find special witches to unclamp your wheels in the green and black pages of the Yellow Pages.

5

You must bring the witch lots of chocolate. Witches like Green & Black's organic chocolate best. Young witches (like me) prefer the cherry flavour. Older witches (like auntie) love the mint or butterscotch flavour. Very old witches prefer the almond, ginger, or just plain dark chocolate (to match their plain dark clothes) if they've got any teeth! You can buy this chocolate at Sainsburys. If you are rich, the witches like an expensive present; gothic jewellery, black velvety clothes, or a new shiny cauldron.

Auntie's friends gave her lovely birthday presents: elderflower and rose petal jelly, dandelion wine, a herb pillow, gingerbread men, Green &

Black's chocolate, candles from M&S (Magic and Spells) and a witchy top from WHS (Witch's Home Stores).

We watched Hocus Pocus because auntie's friends had borrowed her Harry Potter DVDs. We ate some of the chocolates I gave auntie. She said witches are often toothless with a big spot on their nose because they love chocolate so much. I chose the Strawberry Bloom (real strawberries nestle with a sweet, strawberry fondant) and the Orange Blossom (dark chocolate protects this precious orange nectar centre). Auntie said, 'Who writes this stuff?!' She cackled and decided to try the Midnight Praline (a whole roasted

hazelnut hides in a velvety dark praline). Auntie chose this chocolate because witches are often nutty and like to hide inside a dark velvety cloak. Then she ate the Roasted Nut Harvest (smooth hazelnut praline draped in rich dark chocolate) and said she was going to try not to finish the whole box when I went home. I chose some chocs to take home and auntie wrapped them in cling film. She wraps lots of things in cling film, I think it's one of her hobbies.

When auntie was in the bathroom I had another peek in her wardrobe. If you climb inside (leaving the door open of course) you can visit the land of Narnia, if you are lucky, and wish really hard. I wished hard but nothing

happened. Mum says, third time lucky, so I will try again twice. I might find myself in a forest with snow on the ground and meet a friendly fawn under a lamp-post. I don't want to meet the bad witch who turns animals into stone. I hope I get home in time for tea!

One of auntie's friends rang her on her mobile phone to wish her a happy birthday. They did a lot of cackling. Auntie said, 'The more chocolate you eat, the better you cackle!'

Her mobile is a Motorola phone and she uses a T-Mobile service provider. The T stands for Tree. You don't need to re-charge a Tree-Mobile using power from electricity, you just place the phone next to a tree trunk for an hour. If you do this at full moon all your calls and texts to wizards and witches are free for two weeks. Auntie said, 'This is an environment-ally friendly practise because the trees aren't sapped of energy and the moon loves you to use it's magical powers.'

If it looks like it's going to rain, auntie wraps her phone in cling film before placing it under a tree. She never leaves it out in strong sunlight, frost, hail storms or thunder storms. Once she couldn't find it because she couldn't remember which tree she had put it under and the ground was covered in three inches of snow.

Sometimes her phone bill is quite big because the naughty pixies steal her phone from under a tree to text their pixie pals. Now and then, the fairies borrow her mobile to phone fairy family and friends. Auntie doesn't mind this, if the pixies leave her a beautiful bindweed basketful of freshly picked berries and the fairies leave a fabulous fairy  fragrance made from freshly squeezed pink rose petals. They pour the fragrance into an empty snail shell and the spiders seal it with spider web. I think that's why auntie always smells so nice.

I had another look at the long cloak with a silver lining in the wardrobe while auntie was cackling on her mobile phone. It felt ever so nice and soft. There were lots of green bats and purple frogs embroidered on it, with sequins for eyes. There midnight blue and crimson velvet dresses, black spider web lace tops, a long

purple skirt with tassels and a black velvet jacket with a silver dragon broach. In the bottom of the wardrobe I found lots of pairs of shoes and boots, mostly black or purple. A pair of boots had luminous spider webs on. A pair of silver shoes had blue moons and stars on. Another pair was bright green with ivy on. Auntie has small feet, size three. She is the same size as me, so I'm going to ask her if I can borrow the silver pair, when I dress up for Halloween.

Some of the pairs of boots and shoes in the bottom of the wardrobe looked new and shiny with very high heels and pointy toes. I secretly tried them on. They looked lovely but I fell over. I didn't hurt myself because I fell onto the bed. Auntie said, 'Those high heels are impossible to walk in, but I just had to have them because they're so witchy. Your feet dangle in the air anyway when you're on a broomstick!'

I asked auntie why some pairs of shoes had a right or a left one missing. She said she had lost the odd one whilst flying to a party. I cackled and said that I didn't think people would expect to see a witch on a broomstick wearing high heeled pointy designer shoes. Auntie said they look really cool with her 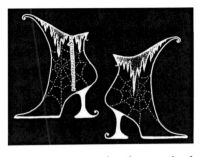 designer-pointy-hat and super-sequin-bag tied to her broomstick. They are the latest fashion must-have in Weekly Witch magazine.

Auntie is writing an article for Weekly Witch magazine about the sort of chocolate witches love best. The title will be, WITCH CHOCOLATE. She has just finished an article about how to make magical soup for Witches' Kitchen Monthly. The title will be, WHERE THERE'S A WAND THERE'S A WAY. Last month she wrote a short story for the young witches' magazine, Cackle. The title was, WHERE THERE'S A WITCH THERE'S A WAY.

Sometimes auntie forgets to put shoes or boots on and rides her broomstick wearing her witchy slipper socks. They were knitted for her

by a witch called Mary Dempster who lives in Creetown, Scotland. The wool is thick and black with sparkly silver bits, they look very magical!

We are going to do some spells using herbs and candles. When we do a wishing spell I am going to wish for a broomstick, like the ones in the Harry Potter films (a Nimbus 2000 or a Firebolt). Auntie is going to wish for M.E. to be taken more seriously.

I saw written in her spell book: An ye harm none, do what ye will. What ye send forth comes back to thee.

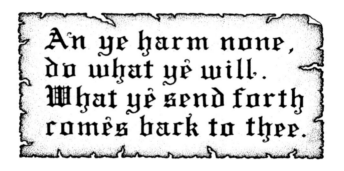

An ye harm none,
do what ye will.
What ye send forth
comes back to thee.

Sometimes auntie calls her spell book the Book of Shadows. It is as big as a cushion and heavy, with a midnight blue cover. There are drawings of silver moons and stars, potion jars, herbs and strange animals on the cover. They seem to move if you stare at them for a long time. Auntie says that's because they can feel the magic simmering and bubbling within the pages. At full moon she has to put the book in the fridge because it gets overheated with excitement and she can't pick it up.

The heat makes the milk curdle. The Edam cheese turns into tiny cheese cows and they wander around the fridge mooing. Their baby bells tinkle. Miniature hens hatch from eggs and start clucking. The top of the horseradish sauce unscrews and a little white horse pops out, he whinnies and gallops about wildly. The orange juice carton turns into oranges. The cucumber thinks it's a cricket bat and hits the tomatoes and oranges so they bounce off the fridge walls. Lettuce leaves shake with fright and scream. Herbal potions bubble and fizz and sometimes the corks pop out.

Auntie must have the noisiest fridge in the world! She would like one with a see-through door so she can sit in her kitchen and watch the magical things happening if there's nothing on TV.

There's a poster of a scary black cat on the kitchen wall. When magical things happen in the fridge, the cat blinks his eyes!!

Chapter Two

Chocolate Frog Cookies

Last week I was teased at school because I am so slow at running. I wrote to auntie and told her. She said I should tell the bullies that she is going to put a spell on them to make their toes drop off if they don't leave me alone. I'll tell them she will do the spell by mixing toe-nail of bat (a clipping from a bat who likes neatly trimmed toe-nails) with melted green candle wax. She will carve the bullies' names on green candles before melting them in an old cauldron. The names will be sealed with frog spit (the frogs are happy to spit for her because they are her friends). Then she will sprinkle owl drop-pings into the cauldron, collected by the fairies. She rewards them with Tesco fairy cakes because collecting owl droppings is not a nice job. After this auntie will light a green candle (made from the melted wax) and say lots of magical words.

If this warning does not work auntie will dress up in her long

black cloak with the silver lining, pointy black hat and high heeled witchy boots. Then she will stand at the school gates staring with a very scary witchy squint.

Auntie said she will enjoy doing an enormous loud sniff with her nose in the air, like she is sniffing out naughty children. She said bullies smell like dog's poo! There will be a friendly bat sleeping in her pocket. It might fly around her pointy hat a few times for a good effect, if it gets excited. In her handbag auntie will have a dictaphone with recordings of giant slimy child-eating toads. She is thinking of playing it loudly so that the bullies will think the toads are going to jump out at any moment!

Dad has ordered me three books: Battling Broomsticks, Witch in Training and The Party Pony. Mum takes me to pony riding lessons on Sunday. I have fallen off

my pony three times, but I wasn't hurt. Auntie
has fallen off her broomstick at least ten times
but she doesn't fly very high. Sometimes she
is lucky to land in a tree or a hedge but when
she falls into a pond it is horrible and cold and
wet AND she has to spend ages saying sorry to
the frogs and fishes.

Last week auntie fell on top of a garden
gnome. He was fishing in a ~~nabor's~~ neighbour's
pond. His head broke off! This made the fairies
cry (and her neighbour) so she brought the
gnome home and stuck his head back on with
Bostik glue. Auntie painted his jacket bright red
and his trousers bright blue because the
weather had made his clothes fade. He looked
good as new. Her neighbour has forgiven her
now.

The pony I ride is white and called Storm. Auntie said this is a good name for a witch's pony because witches love storms that go on for hours with lots of fork lightning, it puts them in a good mood for spelling. She doesn't like to ride her broomstick during a storm because her cloak isn't waterproof and it's difficult holding an umbrella over your head whilst riding a broomstick. She said she tried once but ended up hanging upside down. Her pointy hat fell off, so did her black cats, and sweets fell out of her cloak pockets.

Auntie is going to order a very wide brimmed waterproof pointy hat and waterproof cloak from Cackle catalogue. They are quite cheap if you order plain black. The cloaks with silver moons and stars are much more expensive because the fairies have to collect spider webs that have been bathed in moonlit dew.

When they have spun them into web wool, the wool is dipped in silver pixie paint made from the juice of magical mushrooms, silver berries and quartz crystal dust. It takes weeks for the fairies to embroider moons and stars onto the cloaks by hand but the effect is SO MAGICAL.

Sometimes auntie Nettie has to wear two thick scarves, woolly gloves, her M & S (Magic and Spells) thermal underwear and two jumpers when she rides her broomstick at night. She said witches generally prefer to travel by train or car these days but on a broomstick you can hear the wildlife and smell night-time smells. Wood smoke is her favourite smell although chocolate is her most favourite aroma in the whole world. It's mine too!

When I'm a more experienced witch I'm going to learn to ride a broomstick. It sounds fun because bats fly with you and if you are lucky a small owl will perch on your hat and sing to you in owlish, auntie said it's a hoot!

Sometimes she flies with her witch friends. They have given each other funny witchy names: Batina-bat-breath, Potionella-pin-head, Cacklina-claw-toe, Frogella-funny-bone, Cronella-crow-foot and Herbellina-minty-breath. They call auntie, Nettie-numb-bum because that's what she gets when she's been riding her broomstick for too long. Sometimes they call her Ivy because she has lots of ivy plants.

I'm going to call myself Felicity-flyhigh because my black cat is called Felicity and when I have learnt to fly on a broomstick I'm going to go really fast and as high as an aeroplane. I will fly beside an aeroplane and tap on the windows to surprise the passengers. Mum said I will make old ladies faint. She also said, by the sound of things, auntie has been putting too many magic mushrooms on her Tesco mozzarella pizza again!

After school today I watched The Worst Witch. It is my favourite TV programme. It was really good this week. Hettie tried to plan a birthday treat for Mona but it all went wrong because she used a time spell. Miss Cackle made everything alright in the end. Hettie said birthdays are the best thing in the world. I agree!

It's my birthday on the 3rd of July. Auntie is going to give me a special witchy present. She said it will be perfect for Halloween but it will make me cackle anytime.

Auntie Nettie-numb-bum said, when she was a little girl her favourite programme was Bewitched and her favourite film is The Witches of Eastwick. My favourite films are the Harry Potter films, except Harry Potter and the Prisoner of Azkaban because Dad wouldn't let me watch it. He said it would give me nightmares. I got really upset but auntie said he was right because she is supposed to be a grown-up, but it gave her nightmares!

We made Harry Potter chocolate frog cookies last Sunday. Auntie pretended to be the grown-up who helps me. I lightly greased the baking tray then emptied the chocolate frog cookie mix into a mixing bowl. I added about five tablespoons of cold water. Then I mixed it all together, to form a dough. We added a little more water, drop by drop and decided to make them magical cookies by dancing around in the kitchen waving our arms in the air. We screeched and cackled like witches when they are broom-stick joyriding. Auntie had to sit down for a rest and to get her breath back. That was her workout for the year.

I sprinkled some flour onto a clean work surface so the dough wouldn't stick. Then auntie showed me how to kneed the dough until it was smooth and workable. I rolled out the dough to about five millimetres thick, then I cut out the cookies using the intender and put them on a baking tray. I placed them well apart because they spread during cooking. Auntie re-rolled the trimmings so we could make seventeen cookies.

I put the oven on gas mark five and auntie put the cookies in the oven. While we waited for ten minutes for the cookies to bake we made up a song.

COOKIE SONG

Bake, bake
Bake, bake

Chocolate cookies
For your break

Frog, frog
Frog, frog

Little treat
For your dog

I wrote the bit about the dog and the frog.

Auntie took the cookies out of the oven and we let them cool for a couple of minutes. We made up another song.

COOKING COOKIES

When the tray
Is lightly greased
We'll be ready
For our feast

Oven is on
Gas mark five
Chocolate frogs
They seem alive

They will hop
Around the room
We'll have to
Chase them
With a broom

We put the cookies on a wire rack to cool a bit more before decorating them with icing eyes. I LOVE baking cookies.

I noticed a pair of wizardy boots by auntie's back door. I asked her who they belonged to and her face went as red as her strawberry jam. She said a wizard friend had given them to her for gardening. But auntie doesn't have the energy to do any gardening!

There was also a pointy hat with a very wide brim and a big **W** on it. When I asked if it belonged to auntie's wizard friend she went as red as her tomatoes. I tried it on and it fell down over my eyes. Auntie's wizard friend had lent the hat to her for when she rides her broomstick in the rain. It's like a pointy umbrella. If you leave it outside in the day it becomes luminous at night. This attracts the luminous dragons who will guide you on a long journey.

The hat has a bell on it too. If you shake your head before landing in the woods this warns the

night-time wildlife to take cover in case you land on their heads. If you're in town this warns policemen in case you land on their heads. Auntie sometimes straps a torch to her broomstick and screams, 'WATCH OUT! WATCH OUT!' This usually does the trick.

Chapter Three

Hop... Skip... Fly...

Spun silk the moon looks down.
Babs my cat looks back and ponders.

I sent this verse to auntie in my last letter and she cried happy tears, she says I'm going to be a lovely witch. Mum says sometimes my letters make auntie cry but I don't write anything sad in them. Mum says it's because they make auntie happy.

Spun silk the moon looks down

Babs my cat looks back and ponders

I went to a wedding with Mum and Dad and my brother Matthew. Mum cried. I don't know why, because the bride looked beautiful in her

28

big white wedding dress and she didn't get it dirty. I saw the bride cry too. Maybe her new shoes hurt her feet. Auntie said the bride had probably just realised that she'd made the biggest mistake of her life. Mum said, looking at the in-laws, this was probably true.

I threw a whole box of confetti at the bride and bridegroom after the wedding. On Sunday auntie gave me another box of confetti to throw over my toy prince and princess when they get married in my dream fairy castle.

Auntie prefers black witchy confetti to the pastel coloured confetti. Witchy confetti has bats, stars, frogs, spooks, bells and hearts. It's not just for a witch's wedding, it's fun to throw at Halloween when you go trick-or-treating!

My dream fairy castle is pink with purple turrets and plays tunes. Auntie would love to live in a pink fairytale castle with purple turrets and lovely fairy music playing all day. She would like a cook, maid, and a gardener too; then her hands wouldn't ache so much and she could play her guitar more often. She likes to play drums and percussion too because witches love a good beat.

There are lots of different drums in auntie's spare room. Some are African and her favourite is the Irish one, called a bodhran.

One day auntie will have the energy to play her drums again. She is not sad because the fairies sometimes visit her and tap dance for fun

on her drum heads. They do Irish dancing on her Irish drum and this makes her cackle. Sometimes a passing leprechaun will visit and do a bit of dancing too.

Auntie's drumsticks are magical! They look like ordinary drumsticks but when she taps a little rhythm on her cauldron magical things happen; the steam from her witchy soup swirls into rainbow colours, sparkly spirits appear making spooky squeals, then disappear up the chimney. Auntie calls this soup, bubble and squeal.

Last time I visited auntie she sang, 'The rhythm of life is a powerful beat, feel it in your fingers, feel it in your feet.' Then she said witchy things like, dance allows us to commune with our own spirit and the Spirit. I hopped around pretending to be a frog.

We decided to make a fairy ring to dance in, with lots of Tesco fresh button mushrooms. We put the mushrooms in a big circle on the living room carpet, then we danced and made up songs. Auntie was too tired to dance for long so she did a witchy wiggle.

HOP... SKIP... FLY...

Hop, hop
Hop, hop
Wish I had
A lollipop

Sing, sing
Sing, sing
Dancing in
A fairy ring

Skip, skip
Skip, skip
Apple
With a giant pip

Fly, fly
Fly, fly
Broomsticks
In the midnight
Sky

We fell on the floor cackling. That was auntie's exercise for the month. She said spelling wasn't too tiring as long as there wasn't too much chanting involved; pagan aerobics, collecting of herbs in the rain, pouring from heavy jugs, picking up of heavy goblets, picking up of heavy goblins, waving of wands, ringing of bells, anointing this and anointing that, staring at the moon on a frosty night or having to mote this and mote that.

There were lots of herbs floating on the thick green and orange witchy soup in auntie's cauldron. I watched it bubble for ages before we had dinner.

It was made from peas, star shaped carrots, lentils and onions, and smelt very delicious. So did the freshly baked bread. When I tapped on the sides of the cauldron with magical drumsticks, tiny pea green steam dragons appeared, squealing noisily. They breathed out carrot coloured flames then flew round the kitchen twice before disappearing up the chimney. It was SO EXCITING!

The black cat in the poster on the kitchen wall blinked his eyes three times.

After tea we did some star gazing out of the bedroom window. Auntie told me about the Milky Way and galaxies. She said she needs to eat a Milky Way or Galaxy chocolate when star gazing because it takes a lot of mental energy trying to imagine how far away the stars are. We stared at the gaps between the stars and focused on the darkness so we could begin to see stars even further away. Auntie nibbled a bar of Galaxy, I munched a Milky Way.

I read a poem by Frank Dempster Sherman.

DAISIES

At evening when I go to bed
I see the stars shine overhead;
They are the little daisies white
That dot the meadow of the night.

And often while I'm dreaming so,
Across the sky the moon will go;
It is a lady, sweet and fair,
Who comes to gather daisies there.

For, when at morning I arise,
There's not a star left in the skies;
She's picked them all and dropped them down
Into the meadows of the town.

Auntie told me that chocolate is good fuel for riding a broomstick. She said white chocolate is great for daytime journeys, milk chocolate is fantastic for evening adventures and plain chocolate is perfect for midnight travels and Sabbats. She keeps Cadbury's chocolate buttons in a small velvet pouch which is tied to her broomstick. Sometimes there's a bar of Aero hidden in her cloak pocket because the bubbles in the chocolate help a witch to fly higher. Maltesers are good for being a high-flyer too!

Auntie has to hide the Aero bar in a secret pocket in her cloak because there are lots of chocolate loving fairies who will steal it. When you are busy looking where you are going and don't want to crash into a tree, it is easy not to notice them. You can tell when the fairies have eaten all your chocolate when you hear a tiny fairy burp and fairy giggles in your ear. The best thing to do, is to leave a box of Maltesers in a fairy ring with the cellophane wrapper still on, in case it rains. Even if you are tempted to take the wrapper off and eat just one, or two.

Auntie knows a Scottish dragon called Jimmy who has beautiful tartan scales. They are bright red with lots of little black, yellow and green criss-cross lines. He is a Stewart dragon. She hasn't met a dragon from her grandmother's clan, the Gordons, yet. He will have dark green and blue scales or crimson and white. Scottish dragon scales change colour like a chameleon, depending on what they are up to (hunting or showing off).

There is a poem about Jimmy the dragon in auntie's Book of Shadows. She wrote it with the help of her Collins Scots Dictionary. Her wizard friend Jim (from Scotland) sent it to her. I'm going to learn some Scottish words and write them in my Book of Mirrors.

SCOTTISH WORDS

Hogmanay ~ New Year's Eve.
Wee ~ Little.
Dram ~ Whisky.
Bonnie ~ Lovely to look at.
Braw ~ Fine.
Muckle ~ Large.
Mickle ~ Small amount.
Micht ~ Might.
Jeelie piece ~ Jam sandwich.

JIMMY

Jimmy is a dragon
He is tartan, every scale
He comes from bonnie Scotland
With a braw pointy tail

He's a braw muckle beastie
Enjoys a mickle jeelie piece
A wee dram o'whisky
And adores his little niece.

Jimmy likes to fly beside auntie when she rides on her broomstick. She carries extra chocolate buttons for him because dragons love chocolate (especially liqueur chocolates). Sometimes he brings along his mate, Patrick dragon, who has green scales. They are the same colour and shape as shamrock. He comes from Tipperary in Ireland. Auntie flew there on her broomstick before she got M.E., she said it was a long long way to Tipperary.

Jimmy comes from Edinburgh. Auntie said it's not a good idea to travel there by broomstick in winter, even if you're wearing a long thick kilt and thermals. It's best to fly in a warm aeroplane and have meals served on little trays, instead of surviving on chocolate buttons kept in a velvet pouch. If you take your broomstick to Scotland, it's fun to fly up and down Loch Ness (it's fun to fly up and down the aeroplane aisle too, but you get told off!). The Loch Ness monster likes witches and pops out of the water to say hello. If you feed him chocolate buttons he will sing to you.

Auntie showed me the monster's song written in her Book of Shadows. It was written a long time ago by a man called Edwin Morgan.

THE LOCH NESS MONSTER'S SONG

Sssnnnwhufffll?
Hnwhuffl hhnnwfl hnfl hfl?
Gdroblboblhobngbl gbl gl gggg glbgl.
DrublhaflablhaflubhafgabhaflhaFl fl fl
–
gm grawwwww grf grawf awfgm graw gm,
Hovoplodok – doplodovok – plovodokot
– doplodokosh?
Splgraw fok fok splgrafhatchgarb –
lgabrl fok splfok!
Zgra kra gka fok!
Grof graw ff gahf?
Gombl mbl bl –
blm plm,
blm plm,
blm plm,
blp.

Patrick and Jimmy like chocolates with whisky centres best. Patrick loves Bushmill's Irish whisky and Jimmy's nostrils light up when he sniffs Glenfiddich Special Reserve Single Malt Scotch Whisky. He can smell it fifty toad leaps away.

Whisky gives dragons a very good flame when they breathe out spurts of dragon fire. Auntie says it makes their breath very smelly but if she has a wee dram herself she doesn't notice. Patrick and Jimmy get very excited when she gives them chocolate liqueurs on special occasions. They flap their wings madly and make dragon noises, a bit like a horse when it whinnies, but a much higher note.

Auntie takes a box of Celebrations to witchy festivals like Litha and Ostara. When she travels after eight o'clock she takes a box of After Eight mints to give her energy to dance around a fire for half a minute. The chocolate loving fairies can smell chocolate mints twenty frog leaps away so she throws some into the air as she flies along and the fairies have fun catching them.

If auntie's broomstick isn't working very well she takes it outside on a moonlit night and places it in a fairy ring. Then she lays chocolate Matchmakers (mint flavour) on the branches in the shape of a pentacle, whispers a few magical words to the chocolate loving fairies and waves a Matchmaker about like a wand. Indoors, auntie lights a brown candle and watches it burn down whilst eating the rest of the chocolates. Next day the chocolate pentacle has gone and the broomstick has been mended. I'm going to learn how to draw a pentacle.

Auntie loves to stare at the moon. She said that when you're performing a spell the position of the moon is very important.

Full moon ~ healing and empowerment.
Waxing moon ~ growth and new projects.
Waning moon ~ releasing, banishing, cleansing.
New moon ~ divination.

Once we stared at the moon and made up a song. We sang it to the tune of Twinkle Twinkle Little Star. Then I sang, 'Twinkle, twinkle little star, how I wonder what you are.' Auntie had tears in her eyes and said I really am going to make a fine little witch.

LITTLE STAR

Twinkle twinkle
Little star
Magic in
A potion jar
Pick some herbs
And when they droop
Pop them in
Your witchy
Soup

Moon up high
In the sky
Further than
The birdies fly
So very bright
So very true
Cheers you up
When you feel
Blue

I go to music club after school and I am learning to play the clarinet. I know the notes E, D and G. Auntie said it is lovely to have another musical witch in the family and we could form a band one day. We could call ourselves Black Sabbat, The Shiva Girls or The Cauldron Sisters!!!

I have learned that Sabbats are festivals in the witch's calendar. Auntie celebrates Green Sabbats (Yule, Ostara, Litha and Mabon) because she is a green witch. The other festivals are Beltane, Imbok, Samhain and Lughnassadh. Auntie started to tell me about the God and Goddess but her big ginger cat curled up on her lap and snored so loudly it made her feel sleepy. Auntie fell asleep and did a loud witch's snore. I didn't fall asleep but I had a daydream about riding on a broomstick. I was followed by auntie and her witchy friends on their broomsticks, I giggled and woke her up.

I helped auntie take her washing out of the washing machine. She had accidentally put a purple tee-shirt in with white underwear. She said this happened because her old witchy memory and eyesight is failing. I noticed the underwear was the same colour as the flowers on her rosemary plant, a pale lilac. Witches notice that kind of thing and of course we are...

Best Witches

Chapter Four

Fairies and Dreams

Auntie's got a new three piece suite. She bought it from Notcutts garden centre. I'm surprised she got it from a place that sells flowers and trees! Auntie said maybe they grew their chairs from three piece seeds in magical tubs. I said, 'I expect they grow toadstools in magical tubs too.' Auntie cackled, and said she saw a toad sitting under a toadstool once. I told her the toad should have been sitting on it!

Auntie sees fairies. She doesn't see them very often because you have to be in what auntie calls, a magical receptive state of mind. She told  me it's usually children who can see them, but adults who still have childhood wonder see them easily. Auntie isn't very good at being a grown-up but seeing fairies makes up for this. I'm going to look for fairies in my garden.

There is a spell to see fairies in auntie's spell book. It was written in ancient times. Auntie says her witchy cloak is ancient but I think the spell is MUCH older.

SPELL TO SEE FAIRIES

❋ Gather the flowers of roses and marigolds while looking towards the East. Take the petals and soak them separately in spring water for one week. Strain off the petals.

❋ Pour a small quantity of each liquid into a crystal glass bowl.

❋ Add some virgin olive oil, and beat the mixture until it turns white. Then pour it into a glass bottle.

❋ Add hollyhock buds, marigold flowers, young hazel buds and the flowers of wild thyme to the mixture. The thyme should be gathered from the side of a hill 'where the fairies used to go often'.

❋ Add grass from a fairy throne and leave the bottle in the sun for three days for the ingredients to dissolve.

❋ Rub a very little of the mixture on each eyelid and you will be able to see any fairies that are around.

I saw a poem about the rainbow fairies in auntie's spell book. It was written by someone called Anon. I told auntie that I thought it was a weird name and she said the poem was written by a mouse. A nonny-mouse! Then she told me what it really meant and we cackled.

THE RAINBOW FAIRIES

Two little clouds, one summer's day,
Went flying through the sky;
They went so fast they bumped their heads,
And both began to cry.

Old Father Sun looked out and said;
'Oh, never mind, my dears,
I'll send my little fairy folk
To dry your falling tears.'

One fairy came in violet,
And one wore indigo;
In blue, green, yellow, orange, red,
They made a pretty row.

They wiped the cloud-tears all away,
And then from out the sky,
Upon a line the sunbeams made,
They hung their gowns to dry.

Anon

Auntie's three piece suite is very cosy. It is the same colour as purple fruit polos. I told her I'd seen a broken polo on a footpath and two ants were crawling on it. It was in three pieces and I said, 'It must have been a three piece sweet for ants!'

I helped auntie cover her new chairs with witchy throws. They were cotton sheets really, that auntie had tie-dyed. One was green (for balance) another one was yellow (for clairvoyance) and the sofa throw was purple (for intuition and spiritual development). Auntie explained the words I didn't understand.

She has lots of cushions. They are embroidered with frogs, stars, spirals, paw prints, moons and bats. All her cats love to curl up on her new chairs and because they are old, they sleep on them most of the night and day. Auntie sits on the floor now because she likes to see her cats looking happy and contented.

We are going to make dream pillows. They are little pillows stuffed with herbs to put under your pillow. Auntie makes them for her friends and family, with different herbs depending on what they need. A typical herb mix is mugwort, rosemary and hops, or lavender, mugwort and rose. I have written all this down in my spell book which I call my Book of Shadows. Auntie said, with a witchy stare, 'I like to use the phrase, Book of Shadows because it suggests that the contents explore the dark recesses of our subconscious.' Then she told me what she meant. I am going to press flowers and herbs and write poetry in my Book of Shadows. Auntie said, with another witchy stare, 'Some witches call their spell book a Mirror Book because it reflects their innermost thoughts.'

I said, 'I could call my spell book a Book of Mirrors.' I could stick one of mum's handbag mirrors on the front cover. Dad has lots of mirror tiles in his shed, I could use some of them too. I'll practise my witchy stare a lot and do witchy make-up. Auntie said, 'You really are turning into a Best Witch.' I said, 'Better than turning into a frog!'

I am looking forward to making dream pillows. Herbs for dreaming should be collected during a waxing or full moon. When I write this in my Book of Mirrors I am going to glue some dried herbs onto the page too. Auntie has already got lots of dried herbs in her airing cupboard that she collected at a waxing moon. She said a friendly magical owl helped her. He perched on her shoulder and his eyes were like little torches, so she could see the herbs in the dark.

Auntie showed me a poem in her Book of Shadows that her wizard friend Len had sent her.

DREAMS

**If I had a penny I'd buy me a cat
With big green eyes – and very fat
If I had a shilling – I'd buy me a coat
With big brass buttons – and live on a boat
If I had a pound I would buy me a horse
With a suit of armour and sword of course**

**But if I had a wish
I would give it to you**

**Then you could make all your
dreams come true.**

It's best to use cotton for the dream pillows because it's a natural plant fibre. We are going to use different coloured cotton too, like pink for love and white for meditation. Auntie said meditation is a good thing to learn if you have M.E., if you have the energy to learn anything. She said just sitting in her herb garden, rubbing a rosemary leaf between her fingers and smelling the herby scent helps her to relax.

We are going to make an amber coloured pillow for me because amber will help develop my witchy skills. Then we'll make a blue and purple one for auntie because these colours are for health and healing. I read in auntie's Book of Shadows about making little bags to fill with herbs that you can put in your bath.

FOR ENERGY

Heather
Lemon balm
Rosemary
Savory

FOR PEACE

Chamomile
Hops
Lavender
Peppermint
Rose

There are lots of herbs in auntie's garden. She told me all their names then she started singing, 'Parsley, sage, rosemary and thyme.' She said the words are from an old song by Simon and Garfunkel and she will play it on her guitar for me and teach me the words.

Auntie likes to water her herbs when she has the energy, but she never has the energy to mow her lawn. The grass is often so long that you can hardly see her cats. They look like tigers, black panthers and leopards in the jungle.

I asked auntie if she grew magic mushrooms. She said she doesn't because they give you a headache and make you think you're flying on a broomstick when you are not. They also make you think you can sing when you are out of tune! She much prefers Tesco's fresh button mushrooms and Sainsbury's closed cup chestnut mushrooms.

Before tea auntie told me about making a witch's wand. I wrote some things down in my Book of Mirrors. Wands are made from lots of different trees. Apple is for love and spirit food, vine for happiness and alder for water magic and strength. Auntie is going to make me a wand out of poplar to help me pass my exams when I'm older. She has a wand made out of willow.

Willow is also known as the witches' tree, a moon tree. It is used for protection, moon magic, healing, love, divination and friendship. Auntie would like to wave her wand over everyone in the world who has M.E. to make them feel better. Also she would like to take cauldrons of potato and onion soup to people all over the world who are bed-ridden with M.E. because it is good for making the immune system strong. She would give them all a big healing witchy hug too.

I helped auntie to make potato and onion soup because she was feeling very tired. I did a lot of the chopping because her hands ached. Auntie didn't like to see me using a sharp knife so she did a quick spell to stop me from cutting my finger. While she waved her wand, she said in a witchy way, 'Notcutts, Notcutts, no cuts, no cuts, safe as houses, warm as trousers.'

We made up a song while the soup was bubbling. As I sang the song I tapped a beat on the side of the cauldron with auntie's wand and magical things started to happen!

WITCHY SOUP

Peel, peel
Chop, chop
Bubble, bubble
Pop, pop
Potatoes, onions
Parsley too
Hubble bubble
Brew and brew

Tap your cauldron
With a wand
It becomes
A magic pond
Multi-coloured
Sparkly steam
Dragons are
A witch's dream

Round and round
They fly and flare
Mind they don't get
In your hair

The swirly steam turned rainbow colours and sparkled. Ten tiny steam dragons with onion and potato coloured scales hatched out of bubbles when they popped. They made a loud buzzing noise as they whizzed around the kitchen ten times, VERY EXCITING!!! When they went up the chimney I didn't feel sad because auntie said she has lots more surprises in store for me.

Witches love tiny soup dragons because they are so funny and friendly. If you are flying over a chimney when it's dark, and they are flying out of it, they will greet you with jets of rainbow fire that light up the sky like miniature fireworks. That's why auntie has some tiny burn marks in her old witchy clothes.

In November, when lots of people are having firework parties, auntie and her witchy friends love to send soup dragons up the chimney for fun. This makes up for not being able to go out on their broomsticks because it's dangerous to fly when people are setting off fireworks.

When the soup dragons had flown up the chimney, the black cat in the Chat Noir poster on the kitchen wall blinked his eyes ten times.

CHAT NOIR

Spooky cat with spikey fur
Sees the cauldron as we stir

With a wand I tap a beat
I'm sure I saw him tap his feet

I wrote Love and Best Witches at the end of my letter to auntie and put a kitten sticker on the envelope because she loves cats, she has six!!!!!! Three are from the same litter. The other

three adopted her because, she says, cats know a lovely comfortable witch's home when they see one because they are very sensitive intelligent animals.

Auntie doesn't mind when her kitchen is covered with muddy paw prints, she likes the shape of them even though sometimes she is too tired to clean them away.

Her biggest black cat likes to stand on her legs before he curls up on her lap and he often leaves paw shaped bruises. Auntie loves them, and is sad when they fade away. Once she drew around them with a felt pen so they lasted longer.

Auntie's cats have witchy

names. Her male black cats are Thor, Pentacle and Equinox. Her grey female cat is called Litha, her ginger cat is Solstice and the tabby female is called Samhain. They like to take turns riding with her on her broomstick, on special occasions.

63

I gave auntie cat socks last Christmas. I gave her three pairs. They were black, pink and purple. Auntie said, 'They are purpley, purrrfect for a cat loving witch.' She likes to wear them on cold broomstick riding nights under her boots. On warm summer evenings she rides barefoot with her toenails

painted purple. She said if it suddenly turns cold her feet turn purple too!

If her feet are ticklish, it means she's flying too near the treetops. Friendly bats sometimes fly with her and tickle her feet or a passing dragon nibbles at her toes for fun. Once the flower fairies made daisy chains and hung them round her ankles.

Most of auntie's socks have pictures of frogs on them. She likes to wear them because they put a spring in her step for two seconds. One of her favourite pairs has toads on. She said, 'They are toadily cool!' They were given to her by her witchy friend,

Frogella-funny-bone. Her other favourite pair have a picture of witch. I gave them to her last Halloween. She said, 'They are well witchily wicked.'

Auntie has socks with the days of the week on them too. She likes to wear the right pair on the right day. Sometimes she wears a Monday sock and a Tuesday sock, when it's Friday. Or Wednesday socks at the weekend. She said, 'It makes me feel exciting, wild and daring!'

I told mum and she said, 'That witchy sister of mine is sad.' Then she cackled because

I have taught her how to cackle really well.

We danced around the kitchen screeching and cackling. Our dog jumped around and barked. Dad said, 'What WILL the neighbours think!'

I have a tee-shirt with a witchy hat drawn on the front and one with paw prints on. Auntie drew them both for me using a fabric pen. She drew pictures on tee-shirts for her witchy friends too. Batina-bat-breath wanted bats and Frogella-funny-bone wanted frogs, of course!

Auntie has a collection of doll's tee-shirts, they are lots of different colours. She said, 'I used to take some of them with me, in my cloak pockets, when I flew on my broomstick on frosty nights. You would be sur-

prised how many little dragons get shivery when they fly with you on a cold night. They love to wear brightly coloured tee-shirts, so they can show off to their friends.'

Some of the flower fairies love pink, white and yellow Barbie tee-shirts, with glitter on. Auntie said, 'I call them the bling fairies.'

There is a picture on auntie's kitchen wall of black cats with their tails in different positions. Under each cat it says what the position means. It's written in French so auntie can't understand it, but she can guess what chagrin and la décision means. She said a witch always knows what her cat is trying to tell her anyway.

LE CHAT DOMESTIQUE et SON CARACTÈRE

L'INDIFFÉRENCE

LA DÉCISION

LA BONNE HUMEUR

LA COLÈRE

LA JOIE COMPLÈTE

LA FRANCHISE

LA RUSE

LA MÉFIANCE

LE CHAGRIN

LA JOIE   LA PARESSE   LA FLATTERIE

Chapter Five

Snails & Halloween

On Friday I watched The Worst Witch, it was really good. Hettie tried to win the golden broomstick but it was awarded to Dylis Mustardseed who had done a very clever spell. She had turned a dog ornament into a real dog! Belladonna stole the golden broomstick from her so she could open the witch's portals to let bad witches into the school. The bad witches were going to do lots of bad magic but Miss Cackle saved the day again with the help of the girls.

Sometimes I watch a programme called Witch. It's a cartoon with five witches and their names spell out the word WITCH.

Will
Irma
Taranee
Cornelia
Hay Lin

I like Will best, she is the head of the W.I.T.C.H. gang. Auntie likes Irma because she says Irma reminds her of me when I'm dancing around pretending to be a witch.

My friend Molly has named all her pets so they spell out WITCH too.

Wanda the goldfish
Isabella the other goldfish
Thomas the ginger cat
Charcoal the black cat
Harry the hamster

Auntie has named five snails that sleep behind one of her flower pots.

Simon
Nigel
Andrew
Ian
Leonard

I asked auntie how she knew they were boy snails. She said they were such handsome little creatures with dashing shells. I told mum and she said she still wonders about that sister of hers.

One of auntie's wizard friends is an expert on snails. He said that land snails and most marine snails are ~~hermafrodites~~ hermaphrodites (male and female!). Some freshwater and marine species are boys or girls.

Auntie loves snails. She thinks they are fascinating little creatures. In the summer she puts lettuce out for them. At about nine o'clock they appear for a feed, there's about twenty of them. Auntie likes to kneel down and listen to them crunching on the leaves. I gave her a toy snail for Christmas (Brian the snail) from The Magic Roundabout. She collects toy snails and garden ornament snails.

When auntie was very ill, years ago, it took her ages to crawl up the stairs. She was like a snail. So she put her toy snails and ornaments on each step of her stairs. They are still there and they make her witchy friends cackle a lot.

Auntie's friend Jim (in Scotland) bought a packet of liquorice snails in Woolworths. The picture on the front of the packet showed a snail with a head and tail. When Jim opened the packet he found liquorice coils with no heads or tails, so he wrote a poem.

DISAPPOINTED SNAIL FANATIC

I bought a bag of liquorice snails.
I look inside and my face pales.
I show them to my wife who wails
'You've been done! These are not snails.
They have no heads; they have no tails.
How can they claim that these are snails?'

The picture on the packet fails
To show that these are coils not snails.
It shows them with both heads and tails,
Eyes and mouth and tentecails.
It breaks all the laws of retail
To pack a coil and show a tail

Would you sell toy trains without rails?
Would you sell cricket stumps sans bails?
Or Monopoly sets without jails?
Seaside spades with no pails?
So why sell coils with no heads or tails
And try to claim that they are snails?

Jim sent the poem to Woolworths weeks ago, but he hasn't had a reply yet. He sent the poem to auntie and she cackled so much that she had to write a poem to send back to him.

DEAR CUSTOMER

We regret you are unhappy
With your sale
A bag of snails without a head!
Without a tail!

To you a promise we must keep
You see, the snails they are asleep
A tiny snore you should hear
If you sing they will appear

73

But we have found
They have some trouble appearing
As it seems this type of snail
Is hard of hearing

We hope you're not too tense
We are sorry, therefore hence
Here's a cheque to cheer you up
For five pounds and fifty pence

Yours sincerely

A. S.

Customer Care Dept.

Happy Halloween!
This Halloween I am
going trick or treating.
What are you doing?

I LOVE Halloween! Last year I dressed up as a witch and mum dressed up as a black cat. She had a long tail sewn onto her leotard. I had a toy black cat on my broomstick called Felicity. I went trick-or-treating with my friends Toby, Shannon, Molly and Courtney. We had a lovely time and got lots of sweets, but it was **VERY COLD**.

Auntie gave me a fright-light for my birthday in July. It's perfect for Halloween because it's a torch with spooky colour filters and chilling sound effects. There's a witchy cackle, creaking door, ghost moan, evil laugh, wolf howl, thunder storm and a help cry.

I've got a trick-or-treat bag with pictures of bats, pumpkins, stars and a ghost on the front. I asked auntie if she went trick or treating with her friends. She cackled and said she was a bit long in the witchy tooth to be knocking on doors for a trick or a treat. Instead she stayed indoors drinking homemade pumpkin wine and watched Most Haunted Live on Living TV for three whole hours!!! The programme was very scary because the witches of Pendle Hill made their presence known by making a table move. Auntie got so scared when she saw the ~~saonce~~ séance that she couldn't finish her pumpkin soup with creepy croutons.

Auntie said, 'My creepy croutons are inedible because they are burnt toast in the shape of creepy crawlies, but they look the part. My bat butties are very edible though. They're chip butties with a bat shape toasted on the top.' Auntie cuts the shape of a bat out of tin foil and puts it on the butties before toasting. She says her bat shapes are a bit crumby!

Dad grows his own pumpkins and makes brilliant pumpkin soup. Auntie says it's wonderfully thick and creamy and delicious. He mixes fried onions, garlic, salt and pepper with the pumpkin. Witches would travel hundreds of miles in all weathers to taste it!

Auntie is going to watch Jamie Oliver on Channel 4 because he's going to make pumpkin winter salad, pumpkin soup, and delicate pumpkin fairy cakes.

Last time I visited auntie we made orange, coriander and carrot soup. We made up a song too.

MAGICAL SOUP

Hubble bubble
Witchy stew
Carrots, onions
Brew and brew

Crushed up seed
And orange rind
Coriander
Hard to find

Fry the veg
In butter soft
Bats are stirring
In the loft

Add the water
And the seed
Boil, then simmer
At slow speed

Blend with juice
When it's full moon
Stirring with
A magic spoon

While we sang our song I stirred the bubbling soup with a magical wooden spoon. It had carvings of strange spooky symbols on the handle. Auntie tapped the side of the cauldron lightly with her wand and the rising steam turned bright purple. Then it turned deep blue and tiny orange bats (the size of baked beans) popped out of bubbles. They were screeching wildly and there must have been hundreds of them!!! It was a bit scary at first, but fun when they flew round and round the kitchen for ages. They were like a swarm of angry bees, but auntie said they were happy Halloween bats.

The black cats on the French poster were so surprised they started blinking madly, so did the cat on the Chat Noir poster. Auntie said, 'Those blinking French cats get spookier every day.' Then she opened a window so the bats could fly into the garden because they don't like flying up a chimney.

Halloween is when the witches' year begins. Auntie says it's a time when demons and ghosts wander about and witches dance around a fire until dawn. They dance widdershins (the dance of the witches) forming a circle round a bonfire, and dancing in the opposite direction to that of the sun's path around the sky. Sometimes they just do their own thing. Auntie likes to do her own thing. If she has some energy, she wiggles around an electric fan heater to spooky gothic music or the Monster Mash.

I am going to learn the words to the Monster Mash. I will write them in my Book of Mirrors. Auntie sang two verses to me and the chorus.

THE MONSTER MASH

**I was working in the lab late one night
When my eyes beheld an eerie sight
For my monster from his slab began to rise
And suddenly to my surprise**

**He did the mash
He did the monster mash**

The monster mash
It was a graveyard smash
He did the mash
It caught on in a flash
He did the mash
He did the monster mash

From my laboratory in the castle east
To the master bedroom where the vampires feast
The ghouls all came from their humble abodes
To get a jolt from my electrodes

Sometimes auntie makes monster mash to go with her vege-burgers. She mashes potatoes with green peas, shredded purple cabbage and sweetcorn. If she's very tired she uses instant mash and puts black, green or purple food colouring in it.

This year I am going to have a Halloween party at auntie's house. She is not well enough to have a big party, so it will be just me and her. Her friends Potionella-pin-head, Cacklina-claw-toe, Frogella-funny-bone, Cronella-crow-foot, Batina-bat-breath and Herbellina-minty-breath will drop in just for a while. They understand how tiring witchy conversation is for a witch who has M.E. Witches love to chatter and cackle for hours on end about their latest adventure, exciting new spell, or last night's episode of Coronation Street. They will bring lots and lots of wonderful witchy treats.

WITCHY TREATS

Potion fried potatoes
Pentacle peas
Samhain quorn sausages
Cauldron Cumberland veggie sausages
Pumpkin juice
Bat shaped bean burgers
Fermented fun juice
Pumpkin wine
Monster mash
Jumping jelly
Magical muffins
Coven cream
Dragon doughnuts

Chocolate frogs
Spooky sorbet
Magical sparkly apple juice
Harry Potter chocolate frog cookies
Fairy cakes (purple and green icing)

I wrote a poem for auntie, entitled Halloween Party.

HALLOWEEN PARTY

We're going to have a party
With sausages and peas
Drink the juice from pumpkins
Grown on pumpkin trees

We're going to have a party
It will be a dream

Eat lots of dragon doughnuts
Dipped in coven cream

We're going to have a party
With lots of jumping jelly
Play fun witchy games
Because there's nothing on the telly

All the food will be served on black and orange Halloween plates. They will match the orange scrunchies with black felt spiders that auntie and I will wear.

I have the full witch's kit: a broom, three witch's hats, a raggedy dress, a shiny belt, spider web tights (that auntie gave me) a homemade wand, plus some luminous nail polish and black lipstick.

Dad makes fantastic pumpkin lamps at Halloween and we have lots of decorations with spiders, bats and ghosties.

When auntie hasn't got the energy to make a pumpkin lamp she cuts the eyes, nose and mouth out of an orange pepper. When she cuts into the pepper the juice comes out. The eyes look like they're crying, the nose looks like it's running and the mouth looks like it's dribbling! This makes auntie sad for a moment until she sits the pepper in front of a yellow fairy light. The light shines through the pepper and you can see the seeds inside, it's like a tiny magical cave!

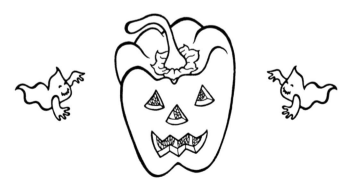

We are going to do apple bobbing and candle magic. We will do the apple bobbing where you try to pick apples out of a bowl of water with your teeth. When auntie was a teenager she did a different sort of apple bobbing. She flew with her friends on their broomsticks over apple trees in an orchard. They rocked the branches of the trees so the apples fell onto the ground, then they collected them to take home. The farmer didn't mind because auntie and her friends made him delicious apple pies.

If a Scottish dragon comes to your Halloween party he will love to join in with the apple bobbing – he will be dookin for apples!

Question: How do you make an apple puff?

Answer: Chase it round the garden.

Auntie told me about candle magic in her last letter. Candles may be used for offerings, meditations, spells and divinations, and something about pausing to remember the Divine within us, which I don't understand. Auntie will explain everything to me when I next see her. Witches don't do magic against other witches, this is something to do with Karmic retribution. I will ask her to explain that too.

I can't see auntie this weekend because she has been overdoing it again. She went to Tesco on her broomstick to buy button mushrooms. It was cold and windy and she wasn't wearing her thermals. Instead of resting when she got home, auntie made winter witch soup with the mushrooms, then did a spell to make the mushroom fairies fly out of the bubbles. She said they did the washing-up for her anyway! Mum said she would like some washing-up fairies. I said, 'We've got Fairy Liquid!'

Beeswax candles are auntie's favourite. We are going to make some by rolling up sheets of beeswax with wicks in the middle. It will be fun! These candles represent the four elements and the spirit. I put a P.S. in my letter to auntie asking if the candles represented the four elephants and my toy horse Spirit too. In her next letter she wrote a P.S.

P.S. In answer to your P.S.
Yes! Cackle! Cackle!
Love and Best Witches x x

Sometimes auntie uses essential oils in her spells. She keeps the oils in jars of all different witchy shapes and sizes. I've written the names of some of the oils in my Book of Mirrors.

ESSENTIAL OILS

Peppermint
Lavender
Tea Tree
Ginger
Lemon
Rosemary
Basil

Essential oils have healing properties. Mum and dad are looking at properties because we are going to move house. I asked mum if she were looking for healing properties and she said, 'What has that sister of mine been teaching you?'

Chapter Six

Healing Spell

When I visited auntie last Sunday I had a cold, and she was sniffing. Her big old ginger cat had been to see the vet the day before because he had a cold too. The vet gave auntie some pink pills to help make him better and he had to be kept indoors in the warm.

I had a red nose. Auntie had a red nose too. Her ginger cat's nose was still ginger. I said we were red nosed witches. Auntie wondered if Rudolf the red nosed reindeer had a very shiny red nose because he had a cold. We shared a big box of Kleenex tissues especially made for little witches with sore noses, they were coated in a lovely balm. I found some oranges in auntie's kitchen and we drew faces on them so they looked like Halloween oranges. Auntie sliced them in half and I squeezed the juice out. Then we made up a song.

ORANGES

Yum yum
Vitamin C
Good for you
Good for me
Praise the Lady
Praise the Lord
If vitamin C
You can afford

Auntie found a healing spell in a very old spell book. The pages were thick, frayed at the edges, smelly and covered in lots of brown age spots. Auntie said they reminded her of some very old witches she knew!

I read out loud from auntie's 'My Fairy Garden' book while she prepared the spell. The fairies were at a wedding banquet.....

'There were strawberry tarts and blackberry jellies, pumpkin pies and buttercup shortbread, angel cakes with sugarplum icing and dandelion lollipops. There was even fizzy elderflower juice which made the youngest fairies sneeze.'

I did a tiny pretend fairy sneeze. It made auntie cackle so much she asked me to do it again but I had to do a big human sneeze instead!

In a pottery oil burner, auntie heated a drop of eucalyptus oil with two drops of lavender oil. Then she lit a tea light in a pottery Halloween spook, just for the witchy effect. We curled up on the new sofa with cats on our laps. I felt nice and warm because I had a woolly shawl (blue with purple pentacles for health and healing) around my shoulders. We made up a poem.

MY CAT

Your purr is
So healing
Your big green eyes
Appealing
You stop me
Feeling blue
With love from me
To you

Your fur is very
Dark
Your claws are very
Sharp
Your nose is very
Wet
You need to see
The vet

The lavender and eucalyptus made us feel very sleepy and relaxed. Auntie's spell book said we should close our eyes and imagine beautiful spirals of golden light. I imagined riding a golden broomstick to Hogwarts School of Witchcraft and Wizardry to meet Harry Potter, Hermione and Ron. Then I rode a golden pegasus to the land of Narnia to meet Lucy, Susan, Peter and Edmund under a lamp-post in a snowy forest.

Auntie had a lovely long daydream. Then she fell asleep and dreamt of finding a big cauldron full of golden coins at the end of a beautiful rainbow. She bought a new kitchen with lots of storage space for all her potion jars and dried herbs, a golden cauldron engraved with magical symbols by the leprechauns of Limerick, a golden broomstick for me that travels to enchanted

lands, and still had lots of money left over to send to A.F.M.E. (Action for M.E.) the M.E.A. (M.E. Association) the R.S.P.C.A., Redwings Horse Sanctuary and the R.S.P.C.W. (Royal Society for the Prevention of Cruelty to Witches).

We drank magical sparkly apple juice and ate Harry Potter chocolate frog cookies and felt much better.

I've seen The Magic Roundabout and I have a toy Dougal, Brian pencil topper and an Ermintrude badge. Dad bought me a Dougal school set. It contains a ruler, pencil, rubber, pencil sharpener and a Pritt-stick. Auntie remembers The Magic Roundabout from when she was a little girl and she liked it when Zebedee said, 'Time for bed, boing!' She still likes to say that now even though she is quite old.

Auntie has a spare room in her house, she calls it the land of Spare Oom. I asked her why, so she found her book entitled, The Lion, the Witch and the Wardrobe, and read to me.....

'Meanwhile,' said Mr. Tumnus, 'it is winter in Narnia, and has been for ever so long, and we shall both catch cold if we stand here talking in the snow. Daughter of Eve from far land of Spare Oom where eternal summer reigns around the bright city of War Drobe, how would it be if you came and had tea with me?'

In auntie's Spare Oom we found lots of books that she had when she was a little girl. I read out loud from The House at Pooh Corner. I read about Tigger because auntie was wearing Tigger socks. She said they put a spring in her step and make her feel bouncy for five seconds. She wished they lasted longer!

'I'm Pooh,' said Pooh.
'I'm Tigger,' said Tigger.
'Oh!' said Pooh, for he had never seen an animal like this before.
'Does Christopher Robin know about you?'
'Of course he does,' said Tigger.

Auntie read a poem to me that her friend Jim had sent her from Scotland.

CHRISTOPHER ROBIN ONLINE

**Little boy looks for the ideal web page.
Downloads an essay, it's all the rage.
Gets top marks. This lad's no fool.
Christopher Robin is cheating at school.**

**Where's Nannies dressing gown? It is no more.
It used to hang on a hook by the door.
But now it's gone. Vanished away.
Christopher Robin sold it on Ebay.**

**Played the stock market on the internet.
Made a small fortune but not finished yet.
Hush, hush, whisper who dares.
Christopher Robin is trading his shares.**

Wee fingers tapping on computer keys.
Nanny won't tell him of things like these.
Eyes glued to the flickering screen.
Christopher Robin's found something obscene.

He copies movies from the internet.
Sells them down the market, his best idea yet.
Money rolls in. How can it fail?
Oops! Christopher Robin has landed in Jail.

We cackled a lot, then I read a bit about Christopher Robin in The House at Pooh Corner.

'Pooh!'
'Yes' said Pooh
'When I'm – when – Pooh!'
'Yes, Christopher Robin?'
'I'm not going to do Nothing any more.'

Auntie says you have to learn to be good at doing Nothing when you have M.E. She is much better than she used to be, so she is not doing Nothing any more.

100

I found a box of get-well-soon cards. They were given to Auntie when she first got M.E. seventeen years ago. Her favourite ones are on a shelf, covered in cobwebs.

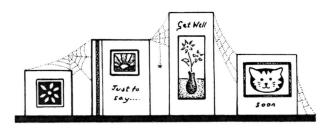

One day, when auntie has got more energy she is going to pop on her thermals, warm woolly big knickers, long thick kilt with a fancy pin, best wide brimmed pointy hat, pointy boots (with high heels that she can't walk in but look good on a broomstick) water-proof cloak (with inside pockets for useful things like Maltesers, Aero, a walkman and map) and ride on her broomstick to Scotland.

I reminded auntie that she must not forget to tie a velvet pouch to her broomstick, filled with chocolate buttons for a dragon and Nessie (who lives in Loch Ness) so he will sing to her.

Auntie will take Jimmy the tartan dragon to meet Nessie and her friend Jim. Jimmy dragon and Jim like to try out different whiskies so they will have something in common to talk about. Because Jim is Scottish and very interested in wildlife, we think he will know how to speak Scottish Dragonish.

I am going to learn Scottish Dragonish. I have written some words in my Book of Mirrors. Auntie said dragons are very polite unless they decide to fry your head off. It's best not to make them angry, give them whisky and smile a lot.

It's a good idea to tell them a joke so they can show off by snorting a bright happy flame. You must stand well back. They like jokes about the English, Irish and Scottish dragons going into a pub. But don't tell those jokes to a Welsh dragon because he will feel left out and probably fry your head off!

SCOTTISH DRAGONISH

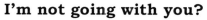

How are you?
Hayyy Munnnn Fitttlikeesss

I'm not going with you?
Ahnnn Naeeee Gyannn Wiyeeeessss

Don't worry.
Dinnnnaaaa Fasshhhhh Yerselllsssssss

It's a fine bright moonlit night for dragons.
Itssssaaaa   Brawwwbrichttt   Minlichtnicht Frrrrrrrrmuckle Beastiessssss

Chapter
Seven

Umbrella Spotting

Auntie supports Redwings Horse sanctuary. Her letters are sometimes written on horse notelets or cat writing paper, from their gift catalogue. She is going to order a pink Dozy Mares sweatshirt for me from Redwings, with sound effect (if you press a button on the front it goes neigh, neigh, neigh). For herself, she is going to order a brown Naughty Nags half zip polar fleece because old witches sometimes turn into naughty old nags!

We looked at the Redwings catalogue and liked the umbrella with pictures of wild horses running all over it. Mum said she needed a new umbrella because her old one is broken. I think she would like one with horses on because she comes horse riding with me on Sundays now.

Dear Louise

I hope you like my new writing paper! I ordered it from Redwings Horse Sanctuary.

I have found a new exciting spell in a very old spell book. I can't wait to tell you all about it!!

Love and Best Witches Auntie Xo

Auntie would like to ride horses too if she had the energy, but she can ride her broomstick because it takes much less effort.

Auntie was well enough to go to the Dickens Festival in Rochester this year. There was a stall there selling umbrellas with all sorts of lovely pictures on them: cats, dogs, horses and paintings by famous artists. Auntie said it was very exciting because she likes to collect umbrellas.

When auntie first got M.E. she was only well enough to lay in bed and stare at the ceiling most of the time. When she got a bit better she could sit on a chair and stare out of the window. Her eyes were too tired to read a book or watch TV, so when it was raining, auntie liked to watch the raindrops on the window pane and do umbrella spotting. She said a lot of people had black or plain coloured ones. It was fun to spot a nice flowery or spotty one, for a change.

Sometimes a woman passes auntie's house with an umbrella that has moons and stars all over it. Maybe she is a witch! I've started umbrella spotting. I saw a man with a black one, it had musical notes and treble clefs underneath.

I told auntie and she said he was probably a musician, maybe a piano or guitar player. She thought he may have a tie with musical notes on, a keyring and a mug to match. I asked her how she knew this and she said she'd seen them all in a gift catalogue.

Auntie still likes to do umbrella spotting on a day when she isn't feeling very well. Her favourite ones are golfing umbrellas, the colours of the rainbow.

I've learned all the colours of the rainbow and written them in my Book of Mirrors. Red, orange, yellow, green, blue, indigo, and violet. Auntie

and I made up a poem together about umbrella spotting.

UMBRELLA SPOTTING

Tartan, spotty
Red and blue
Big and flowery
Rainbow too

Moons and stars
Pink and cream
Stripy, dotty
Black and green

White background
Musical notes
Horses, dogs
And cats and boats

Next time I visit auntie when it's raining, we're going to do a spell that makes you fly up into the air while you hold an umbrella over your head. It's the Mary Poppins spell. All you have to do is eat some apple pie. The pie has to be made from apples that have fallen from a tree, after it has been 'bobbed' by a witch on her broomstick. The pie must be made by a witch at full moon, and decorated with pastry moons and stars.

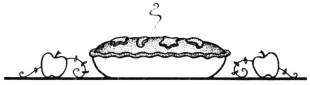

Then you stand outside in the rain with a bat or frog umbrella held over your head with one hand. With the other hand you wave your wand and sing a song. This spell is not suitable for old or very young witches.

MARY POPPINS SPELL

Rise up high, into the sky
Like pastry on an apple pie
Up towards the stars and moon
Whistle a little witchy tune

Be very careful, hold on tight
Or you will get an awful fright
No higher than, the garden shed
Or you may fall and bump your head

Don't stay up high, for too long
Especially when the wind is strong
Landing safely is the key
For Best Witches like you and me

There is a boy called William at my school, he's been teasing me about my imaginary pet dragon. I wrote to auntie and told her about him. She wrote back and said he is just jealous because he hasn't got one. Auntie has some flowers in her garden called snap dragons. If William teases me again, she said I can tell him I've got an auntie who is a witch and will turn her snap dragons into snappy dragons that chase naughty boys and snap at their knees. They will do this when the naughty boys are playing football or running about in games. Snappy dragons are like tiny purple bats. They like to bat footballs away from goalposts. They stop naughty boys from scoring a goal, this makes them more angry than having their knees snapped at.

When I visited auntie last Sunday we found lots of very old spell books in the city of War Drobe. I read out loud from one of them. Some of the words were hard to read so auntie helped me. The books were big and she found them hard to pick up, so I helped her. We took turns in turning the pages over and cackled a lot because I'm really good at cackling now. Auntie said, 'What will the neighbours think?!'

Sometimes the books fly around the house and bump on the walls at full moon. The neighbours think auntie has a ~~poltergiste~~ ~~poltergiest~~ poltergeist. Poltergeist is a German word for noisy spirit.

I saw a book about ghosts with the spell books. There was a chapter about poltergeists. The black and white photo of poltergeist activity was scary because furniture had been thrown about all over the room!

Auntie's friend, Potionella-pin-head, had a poltergeist once. It used to pile books on top of one another. If she left loose change on her table, it made little piles of coins. Potionella-pin-head said she had a neat poltergeist.

We searched for a spell for energy under **E**. Auntie found a chant to help give you energy and connect with your goddess within. I wrote the chant in my Book of Mirrors and I am learning the arm movements too. Mum saw me practising and she said, 'What on earth is that sister of mine teaching you now.' I told her it was called pagan ~~arobies~~ aerobics.

Earth my body
Water my blood

Make hula motion with hands at womb level

Air my breath

Hands reaching up

And fire my spirit

Pass hands over head and clap

I'm going to use lavender picked from auntie's garden in a spell. I can't wait! It will give me courage to stand up to the bullies. I'm going to use basil and mint in a spell too, it will help to bring me more pocket money.

The day before yesterday I found my toy horse Spirit in my toy box. Auntie thought she had lost her spirit once but she found it again. I asked her if she had left it in the land of Spare Oom.

I've seen a picture of witches dancing around a fire. They like to run between bonfires and jump over them for ritual cleansing. The fire jumpers like lots of drums playing. I'm going to practise fire jumping.

Auntie cannot light a fire in her sitting room because her chimney is blocked up. We are going to put an electric fan heater in the middle of the sitting room, I will run around and jump over it. Auntie will tap a beat on one of her drums. She said she is too old for jumping over fires but playing a drum is just as much fun, even if you've only got the energy to tap with a long witchy fingernail.

I've written a fire jumping song in my Book of Mirrors. Auntie is going to make up a little tune to go with it and play it on her guitar.

FIRE JUMPING SONG

**Jumping, jumping
In the air
Silver moonlight
In our hair
Like the fairies
Dancing free
Owls are hooting
In a tree**

Chapter Eight

Hubble Bubble Bath

Yesterday morning mum took me to riding lessons. I fell off my pony again! I didn't break anything but my arm and leg hurt. I went to see auntie afterwards because I knew she would make me feel better.

We had magical sparkly green apple juice and Harry Potter chocolate frog cookies. Then auntie put three drops of lavender oil and two drops of geranium oil in her witchy burner. She said some special words about the Spirit being there to heal me. I closed my eyes and thought about my toy horse, Spirit. Auntie closed her eyes and laid her hands on my bad arm, then my bad leg. Her hands were nice and warm. I felt sleepy and much better.

I had a bath in auntie's bathroom. It's full of spider plants and bright green smiling frogs (not real ones!). On the side of the bath there were funky frog jump-in bath salts, funky frog kissable hand and body lotion, and hip-hop funky frog bubble bath. There was some witchy bubble bath too, called Hubble Bubble Bath. Auntie poured lots of it into my bath, I've never seen so many bubbles in my life!

There were poems on the Hubble Bubble Bath and Werewolf Shampoo.

HUBBLE BUBBLE BATH

Hubble bubble, toil and trouble
Pour the potion at the double
Watch it turn from green to blue
It smells of blueberries and so will you

WEREWOLF SHAMPOO

When the full moon fills the sky
And you hear a werewolf cry
Smell the dewberries in the air
Best stay in and wash your hair

There are lots of little bottles of shampoo and body lotion in Auntie's bathroom. She got them free from hotels when she was on holiday. They remind her of happy days before she got M.E., but she is not sad. There are photographs of the seaside and sealife in the sea too. I like the big frog soap dish best.

I wrote about herbal baths in my Book of Mirrors. To make a herbal bath you put minced herbs in a cotton muslin bag. Then you tie the bag with string and place it in your bath. You can use a ~~combinashon~~ combination of cloves, chamomile, heather, hops, lavender, lemon balm, marigold, mint, pansy, rose, rosemary and savory.

You should think of the herbs giving you energy and making you ever so nice and clean. If you are a very very tired witch you could ask a witchy friend (who has lots of energy) to nip down to the shops and buy you some lavender bath crystals. They do good ones in the Body Shop.

I wrote about the colour lavender in my Book of Mirrors. It is the colour for spiritual development, ~~sikiek~~ psychic growth, divination, sensitivity to the Otherworld and blessings. Auntie helped me with the spelling of the witchy words. When I am a bigger witch I will understand them.

A witchy friend gave auntie some bath pearls in the shape of seahorses and dolphins. She kept some of them because they look nice. There are little plastic fishes, shells, turtles, crabs, starfish and a shark in her bathroom too. Once, auntie put them all in her bath with the bath pearls and pretended to be in the sea. It was the most fun she'd ever had at bathtime.

I forgot to say that auntie has lots of different witchy hair conditioners to make her hair washing day more fun (when she has the energy to wash her hair). She said the excitement of choosing which colour bottle to use, often gives her the energy to wash her hair and keep it in good condition.

Berry Blue ~ For sad witchy hair that has been made flat by a big pointy hat, to give it visible volume and invisible strength.

Dazzling Orange ~ Intense nourishment for witchy hair damaged by too much broomstick riding during cold and wet weather or when damaged by getting tangled in bat wings or chewed by a passing dragon.

Party Pink ~ To lock in hair colour if a witch has dyed her hair purple or green for a party or special occasion like Lammas, Ostara and Beltane.

Frog Green ~ For normal witchy hair which is usually very long, to remove any frog slime if a frog lands on your head.

Egg Yolk Yellow ~ A soothing balm for a blonde witch with a sensitive scalp after too much broomstick riding in strong sunlight.

Robin Red ~ To give warm tones and perfectly defined waves to red hair, frizzled by a passing dragon or chewed by a friendly robin.

Chocolate Brown ~ For smooth silky very long brown hair that tends to tangle in trees.

Coal Black ~ Adds fire to tired black witchy hair.

Misty Grey ~ To add volume and life to flat hair that has endured too many trips in foggy weather.

Plum Purple ~ Gives a fresh fruity fragrance to hair that is smelly after broomstick riding over chimney pots or bonfires.

Snowflake White ~ Gives a bright luminous sparkly glow to any type of witchy hair. This is useful to a witch who travels at night and means she does not need to attach a torch to her broomstick. The luminous dragons are attracted to the luminous witchy hair, they will guide and protect you on a long journey. Singing fairies will also accompany you on your journey to help keep you awake so that you don't get too tired and fall asleep on your broomstick and fall into a tree or down a chimney pot. They will also entertain you so that you will not be tempted to phone your best friend on your mobile for a long witchy chat with lots of cackling.

I like the snowflake white hair conditioner best. I would love bright luminous hair, to match the nail polish I wear at Halloween. I also LOVE snowflakes!

Auntie loves bath things from Lush because they are made from fresh organic fruit and vegetables, vegetarian ingredients and not tested on animals. She especially loves their Snow Fairy shower gel; Squeaky Green shampoo bar, made with nettles, rosemary and peppermint herbs; Coal Face black soap made with liquorice, charcoal and soothing oils; Enchanted Eye Cream, made with lavender, honey and almond oil; and Ceridwen's Cauldron Magical Potion for softer skin, made with oats, cocoa butter and almond oil. Very witchylicious or WITCHYLUSHIOUS!

Chapter Nine

Witchylicious

Today auntie taught me all about Lammas. I wrote everything in my Book of Mirrors and auntie helped me with the spelling of big words. Lammas is the festival of the first of the harvest. A long time ago it would have been a very happy time when men, women and children gathered crops and had a big party afterwards. Lammas has also been called loaf-mass. This reminds us that the first grain and its bread are important.

Lammas is also the festival of Lugh the Sun God, and of the Sacrificial King who is still represented by the gingerbread man. The colours of the festival are golds, yellows and oranges for the God and red for the robes of the bountiful Mother. The bountiful Mother is the Goddess. I asked auntie if the bountiful Mother eats lots of Bounty bars and gets full up!

We made gingerbread men using a rich Esbat biscuit recipe and adding ground ginger. Esbat is the witches' term for full moon meetings or workings.

ESBAT GINGERBREAD MEN

2oz butter
1 tbsp honey
1 egg yolk
3oz plain flour
1oz ground hazelnuts or almonds
Large pinch of ground cinnamon
Large pinch of grated nutmeg
Few drops of vanilla essence or extract
1 to 2 tsps of ground ginger

I had fun helping auntie blend butter, honey, vanilla and egg yolk together until we made a thick paste. Then we mixed all the ingredients together. I added them to the paste until I'd made a stiff dough. After we had chilled the dough auntie rolled it out with her witchy rolling pin. I cut out the gingerbread men with a special cutter.

Auntie put the gingerbread men on a greased baking sheet and we made up a song while they cooked. I made up a witchy dance too, with star jumps. Auntie did a big sunny witchy smile.

GINGERBREAD MEN

Blend butter
And honey
Vanilla
And egg
A ginger arm
A ginger leg
Make a paste
To your taste
Don't worry 'bout
A bigger
Waist

Mix nutmeg
And cinnamon
To a stiff
Dough
Slightly chill
Nice and slow
Cut and roll
Bake golden
And brown
Fit for a king
And his crown

The gingerbread men looked so sweet that we didn't want to eat them. So I found a spell in Auntie's Book of Shadows, under **G**. It was a spell to make gingerbread men come to life!

I did the spell all by myself. Firstly, I poured ginger oil into a witchy pottery burner, then I lit a tea-light under the oil and said the magic words, 'Gingerbread men, gingerbread men, sing and sing, dance and dance, don't just lie there in a trance.' While I said this I tapped each gingerbread man very lightly on his tummy (I didn't want to hurt them) with auntie's wand.

I was so shocked with happiness when all the gingerbread men slowly started to sit up and their smiles got bigger. When they were on their feet they touched hands in a circle then danced round and round on the baking tray. Their feet made a lovely tippy-tappy sound. Then they started singing a happy song and we cackled our heads off. The French cats in the posters on the kitchen wall blinked their eyes wildly!

GINGERBREAD MEN'S SONG

We are happy
It must be said
We are made
Of gingerbread
You can't eat us
That's the catch
You'll have to make
Another batch

Mum buys gingerbread men from Tesco. They look different to the ones auntie and I made because they stand with their arms by their sides. Mum says they look like little toy soldiers. Auntie says they look like Irish dancers standing in a row. If I give a packet of them to auntie next time I visit she will play her magical Irish drum, the bodhran. If I tap a beat on her cauldron with magical drumsticks (while she plays her drum) and we sing about leprechauns too, the gingerbread men will jump out of the packet. They will tap dance in a line, on a baking tray. Their arms will be by their sides like the Irish dancers in auntie's video, Lord of the Dance.

Auntie told me about herb teas. She cannot drink ordinary tea, like Brooke Bond PG tips because it has ~~eafine~~ caffeine in it. If auntie drinks anything with caffeine she turns into a cranky hyper-active witch. She said this is not a pretty sight and we cackled. I danced around pretending to be a hyper-active witch and did more star jumps.

I saw lots of packets of herb teas in a ~~eubord~~ cupboard. The boxes were different colours. I read all the names and wrote them down. Camomile and spearmint, rosehip, nettle, fennel, lemon verbena, peach and passion fruit, blackcurrant and apple, strawberry and mango, banana and cinnamon.

In another cupboard I found lemon and ginger, mandarin and ginger, mango and ginger, and apple and ginger. Auntie said, 'One of those teas will wash a gingerbread man down nicely.'

Some of the other teas taste like wet grass, mouldy fruit, weak jelly, week old jelly, dried flowers or an old wardrobe. We decided to make witchy lemonade. Auntie's lemonade is really cool.

WITCHY LEMONADE

3 lemons
6oz sugar
1½ pints of water
Fairy sparkle juice – collected in a thimble from the dew on spider webs where the fairies live at the bottom of the garden.

I washed the lemons and peeled the rind. Auntie was pleased to have my help because her hands ached. We put the rind and sugar into a heat proof jug and poured boiling water over it. I covered the jug and we waited for it to cool.

I made up a cool witchy lemonade dance. Auntie sat on a chair and closed her eyes. She said she was just resting her eyes and thinking magical lemonade thoughts but I heard her snore. When she woke up she pretended she hadn't fallen asleep.

While I stirred the lemonade auntie tapped the jug with her wand three times. We chanted, 'Lemon rind, lemon rind, magical tree frogs, hard to find. Let them come alive for me, instead of sitting in a tree.' Then we added the lemon juice and fairy sparkle. I strained the lemonade then put it back in the fridge.

After a few minutes we heard strange little bumping noises coming from the fridge. The black cats in the posters on the kitchen wall started to blink their eyes, so I knew something very magical was going to happen soon.

The bumping noises got louder so auntie said it was time to open the fridge door. As soon as she opened it the air in the kitchen sparkled. The whole kitchen smelt of fresh lemons, limes and oranges. Auntie said, 'It's citrusy-witchy-licious!'

Tiny tree frogs (the size of green peas) hopped out of the fridge onto the kitchen floor. They made happy little ribbit noises and went, BOING! BOING! BOING! onto the cupboards, walls, cooker, ceiling, shelves and window pane. They were different colours: lemon yellow, lime green and bright orange.

A lime green frog landed on my nose and made me cross-eyed. Auntie cackled a lot. A lemon yellow frog landed on her head and I cackled a lot too. The bright orange frogs hopped onto our hands then off onto the black bat mobile that was hanging from the kitchen ceiling. They spun round and round, and looked very Halloweenish!

After a while, auntie got tired so she did a spell to send the frogs back to fairy frogland. She waved her wand and chanted, 'Out you go, out you go, we'll miss you so, we'll miss you so. Back to a froggy fairy place, another time, another space.' I didn't feel sad because we can see the magical tree frogs again whenever we like.

I opened the back door and all the little tree frogs hopped out, BOING! BOING! BOING! They made merry ribbit sounds and waved goodbye to us. We drank our homemade lemonade to celebrate, it was very WITCHYLICIOUS.

When auntie fell asleep again I went into her bathroom and peeked in the airing cupboard. I saw her big ginger cat. He was curled up on a pile of towels and snoring loudly.

There was a bunch of dried sage too, tied up with green string. I know about sage. Burning sage makes the air clean and pure. Sage tea helps to reduce fevers and makes your throat feel better if you have an infection.

I'm learning about magical teas. To make tea to help you relax, you need......

1 teaspoon elder flower
2 teaspoons rose hips
1 teaspoon chamomile
2 teaspoons hops
1 teaspoon valerian
1 tablespoon English breakfast tea

Auntie said it is good for a young witch to

learn these things but a nice glass of wine does
the trick for her. All that tea making is for
healthy witches. I saw lots of glasses in her
kitchen cupboard. She said that sometimes she
has fun choosing which one to use because a
change is as good as a rest.

There were two very witchy looking glasses
in a cabinet. They were black and almost twice

the height of auntie's other glasses. She poured some of our homemade lemonade into one of them and lovely things happened. Tiny silvery stars slowly began to appear all over the black glass. They twinkled and sparkled like stars in the midnight sky.

Stars appeared in the eyes of the French kitchen cat posters so I knew something magical was going to happen again soon.

Suddenly the lemonade started fizzing madly, making a very loud hissing noise. I thought the glass might explode! Auntie said, 'Stand well back.' Then hundreds of miniature black and silvery bats (the size of blackcurrants) flew out of the glass and whizzed wildly around the kitchen. They flew around our heads like a swarm of bees, but they were not buzzing. They made very high-pitched squealing sounds. We put our pointy witchy hats on in case bat wings got tangled in our hair. After a few minutes auntie opened a window and they flew outside, into the trees. Auntie said, 'What will the neighbours think!'

When the lemonade stopped fizzing madly I had a sip. Some of the bubbles went up my nose and I sneezed. Tiny stars flew out of my nostrils and we cackled. Auntie had a sip and I saw stars twinkling in her eyes, SPARKLY MAGICAL!!

I saw lots of different egg cups in a cupboard. Some of them were funny. One had a bobble hat to keep an egg warm and one had a witchy hat. Auntie has two boiled eggs for breakfast but once she had three! She wrote a song about them and we sang it to the tune of Three Blind Mice.

THREE BOILED EGGS

Three boiled eggs
Three boiled eggs
See how they run
See how they run

Bought free-range
From a farmer's wife
She greeted me
With a carving knife
Have you ever seen
Such a thing in your life!
Three boiled eggs

Chapter Ten

Dragons & Pentacles

When I visited auntie today she was watching the witches' weather forecast on Sky TV. The weather-witch was wearing a long midnight blue cloak. It had silver sequin clouds, suns, kites, snowflakes, raindrops and lightning flashes sewn all over it. The weather-witch pointed to where we live (on a picture of England) with her wand. She said there would be storms tonight, some sunny spells tomorrow, and the next day would be too windy for flying on a broomstick. Tiny witches on broomsticks flew across the picture of England. They made the sound, wheeeeeee!

When the weather-witch tapped on the clouds with her wand, lightning flashes appeared and there was the sound of thunder. There must have been a wind machine in the TV studio because her cloak flew up in the air and she had to hold her big pointy hat onto her head.

I asked auntie if we could do a sunny

spell and she said, 'Of course!' We found the spell under **S** in her Book of Shadows. Firstly you should light an orange candle. Orange represents the sun, honour, money, power and work. I wrote this down in my Book of Mirrors. I told auntie my favourite colours and she told me what they represented.

PINK ~ Friends, inner peace, fertility, emotional healing, romantic love, self respect.

PURPLE ~ The Goddess as Crone, travel, exams.

TURQUOISE ~ The Goddess as mother, fortune.

If you haven't got an orange candle a yellow one will do for a sunny spell. When you've lit the candle, all you have to do is sip homemade witchy lemonade, then think of a field of sunflowers in the sunshine. This lights up your life!

If witches fly over fields of sunflowers in Northumberland, the flowers lift their heads to watch the witches go by and wave their leaves! This happens because there is magic in the air. The magic leaks out of Hogwarts School of Witchcraft and Wizardry.

I found a rainy spell in auntie's Book of Shadows, under **R**. If you are a tired witch, all you have to do is place a blue candle on a window sill. When it's raining, light the candle and watch the raindrops running down the window pane. If you've got a bit of energy you can breathe on the window pane and draw a pentacle with your finger. It's a very relaxing spell as long as you don't set fire to the curtains. If you are lucky a raindrop fairy will see your candle and tap on the window, then you can make a wish!

I found dragon poems (written by auntie) under **D** in her Book of Shadows.

A DRAGON

I saw a little dragon
Sitting in my chair
He smoked all my fags
After only three drags
Then he coughed
And he frizzled my hair

Auntie doesn't smoke really because it makes your skin crinkle, your hair fall out, and witchy nose drop off. Smoking makes you smell like old witchy slippers too, and cough like a wizard who has smoked a pipe for sixty years. I'm never going to smoke!

MUSICAL DRAGON

A dragon with talons
So sharp
Was sitting and playing
My harp
When he plucked on a string
He flapped a wing
Then in dragonish
Began to sing
What a beautiful dragon
I am, I am

What a beautiful dragon
I am

NOTHING LIKE A DRAGON

There's nothing like
A dragon's stare
He sees into your soul
There's nothing like
A dragon's fire
To set alight your coal

There's nothing like
A dragon's claw
It sinks so very deep
There's nothing like
A dragon's snore
When he is fast asleep

BABY DRAGON

A dragon popped out of an egg
He flew, then he perched on my leg
I decided to call him Norbert
He smiled, then he ate all my sherbet

We had dragon nostrils for tea, but they weren't really a dragon's nostrils. They were pasta parcels filled with cheese and spinach, but they looked like dragon nostrils. We had giant Portabella mushrooms too, from Ireland. Pixies like to shelter under them when it's raining. During sunny spells they like to sleep under them in the shade.

After tea I drew a picture of a dragon. Then I wrote a poem about a witch and drew a witch flying on her broomstick.

Witch, witch

Witch, witch who do you love?
My little sweet mascot, Snowy the dove!
Witch, witch what do you drink?
Heated wolf's blood poured with a clink!
Witch, witch witch, what do you eat?
Those tasty bush leaves down at Plum Street!
Witch, witch where is your broom?
Just at home at the moment, it'll be here soon!
Witch, witch, what do you hate?
YOU ASKING SO MANY QUESTIONS, NOW
BEAT IT, MATE!

141

I learnt how to draw a pentacle too. It's a five pointed star inside a circle. I drew it in my Book of Mirrors using auntie's pencil and compasses. She likes to draw pentacles in salt and in sand at the seaside. I'm going to draw a pentacle in the sand next time I go to the seaside. I will collect pebbles and seashells to make it look pretty, like auntie does.

We made pentacle cookies using the Esbat biscuit recipe. I ate two with a glass of magical sparkly apple juice. Auntie only ate one. She said, 'Old witches have to be careful not to eat too many biscuits and drink only herbal tea, because a fat-old-hyper-active-witch is not a pretty sight!'

I've started to learn about tea leaf reading. It's a very old way of telling fortunes. Auntie didn't have a box of tea leaves in her cupboard so she cut open three herbal tea bags.

Auntie brewed the tea in her witchy teapot. Then she couldn't find her special fortune telling teacup and saucer or her tea strainer. She ate two more pentacle cookies to give her the energy to find them.

We searched for ages, then auntie remembered that she didn't need a tea strainer and Potionella-pin-head had borrowed her teacup and saucer.

When auntie phoned her friend, Potionella-pin-head said she would bring the cup and saucer round in the time it takes a toad to leap twenty five toad leaps. Auntie asked me what time it was. I said it was twenty five toad leaps past tree. We cackled a lot, then we ate more pentacle cookies!

I think Potionella is as forgetful as auntie because as soon as she put the phone down she remembered she'd lent the cup and saucer to Batina-bat-breath. Potionella rang auntie back to say she'd rung Batina but there was no answer, just a message on her answering machine. It said she was out on her broomstick so auntie rang Batina on her mobile phone.

Batina said she'd call back in the time it takes a bat to sing a bat song; this isn't very long.

A BAT'S SONG

**I flutter in the light
Of a great big silvery moon
I sing a batty song
Whistle a witchy tune**

**I fly with the fairies
They smile, they do not frown
And later you will find me
Snoring upside-down**

Batina couldn't speak to auntie when she called because she was riding on her broomstick. It's dangerous to chat on a mobile phone when you're flying on a broomstick because witches like to chatter and cackle for ages, they loose concentration on where they are going and end up in a tree or multi-storey car park.

Before she rang auntie back, Batina landed carefully on a rooftop. She said she had lent auntie's special teacup and saucer to Cronella-crow-foot and would send Cronella a message by

toast. I asked auntie how you can send a message by toast!

Batina does a spell to write a message on toast. Thick white bread is best for this spell – especially Witches' Pride. You must say your message out loud three times, breathe warm witchy breath on the bread and the words will appear. If you have a magic toaster, when the bread is toasted it will fly out of the toaster to wherever you want it to go. You must remember to leave a door or window open or the toast will fly around the house until it finds a letter box or cat flap to escape through.

Witches always know when the toast is going to arrive so they leave a door or window open. Auntie said Cronella likes to stand at her cottage door with her mouth open, ready to catch the toast in her teeth.

Cronella arrived with the cup and saucer in a Tesco carrier bag hanging on her broomstick. She was out of breath and said she had read in the tea leaves that we were thinking of doing the tea leaf reading and needed the cup and saucer. Auntie said, 'Gone off the bloomin' idea now.' But she hadn't really.

Cronella parked her broomstick in the hall. Then she brushed toast crumbs off the front of her cloak. When she hung her cloak up a bat flew out of a pocket. One of auntie's cats tried to catch it, so it flew back into the cloak for safety. Cronella said, 'I've got a bloomin' in-growin' toe nail, I'm parched and me mouth is as dry as the bottom of an owl's cage.' I said, 'I'm perched like an owl on auntie's stool.' Auntie said, 'My mouth is as dry as the herbs in my airing cupboard.' So she put the kettle on.

I poured sparkly magic apple juice for me, then tea for Cronella and auntie. Cronella made herself comfortable on auntie's new sofa. She said the cushions with moons and bats on were nice, the tie-dyed purple throw too. Auntie said, 'It's alright if you want to smoke your pipe as long as you blow the smoke up the chimney in the kitchen.'

Cronella blew smoke rings. They were green. Then she blew purple smoke dragons. THEN she puffed the magic dragons through the smoke rings and they flew up the chimney! I clapped and we all cackled.

I ate another pentacle cookie and Cronella ate five!!!!! She crunched the cookies and slurped her tea in a witchy way. Then she burped and said, 'I like to smoke me pipe and eat lots o'cookies.'

When Cronella went home, auntie and I did some tea leaf reading. Cronella didn't stay for very long because she wanted to hurry home and finish an exciting spell. It was a spell to find a handsome young man who will fall in love with her.

Auntie shook her head from side to side and said, 'That Cronella-crow-foot is after a toy boy again. There's going to be a lot of chanting to the God and Goddess, lighting of pink candles in rose quartz candle holders, and dancing on pink rose petals with no clothes on. At her age, honestly!'

I said I'd much rather have a toy horse than a toy boy. Auntie said I was a very sensible young witch. She gave me her teacup and asked me to swirl the tea leaves round. Then she turned the cup upside down in it's saucer with the handle facing me. With her left hand auntie turned the cup round three times, anti-clockwise. Now the handle was facing her. When I lifted the cup and looked into the saucer I saw a shape, it was a bit like a bell.

A bell can mean good news or a wedding. I've started making a list of symbols in my Book of Mirrors.

ANCHOR ~ A happy ending or a journey.
BELL ~ Good news or a wedding.
CAT ~ Someone is not to be trusted.
DOG ~ News from a friend.
RING ~ Good fortune, an engagement or wedding

When we read the tea leaves again I saw a ring. I've seen a bell too so I think I will be going to a wedding!

It's auntie's birthday next week, she is going to have a birthday party. It will be just for me and her but her friends will come round for a little while to bring her a present. There will be, Potionella-pin-head, Cacklina-claw-toe, Frogella-funny-bone and Cronella-crow-foot. We will have black jumping jelly with green coven cream and blue moon shaped wafers. I'm going to help auntie make bat butties and bat shaped bean burgers. The fairies will bring fairy cakes, magical muffins and pentacle peas. Fairy artists paint a pentacle on each pea with a tiny brush (made from a feather) dipped in nettle juice. Nettle juice is made by the pixies stamping on nettle leaves.

I've written some natural dyes in my Book of Mirrors.

GREEN ~ Coltsfoot and bracken.
YELLOW-GREEN ~ Carrot tops.
YELLOW ~ Turmeric.
ORANGE ~ Onion skin.
RED ~ Madder root.
BLUE ~ Blueberries.
BRIGHT BLUE ~ Red cabbage.

Potionella is going to bring potion-fried-potatoes to auntie's party. Cronella will bring homemade pumpkin wine and lemonade. Frogella will make Harry Potter chocolate frog cookies. I'm going to make bat and frog paper decorations.

Auntie is quite old, she is going to be fifty. Batina-bat-breath looks very old. I asked auntie how old she was and she said, 'Oh, I think she's nearly seventy but she says she's as old as the man she feels, so I reckon that's about twenty seven.'

Instead of playing pass the parcel we are going to play pass the par-snail. A par-snail is a giant party snail with a pretty shell, all the colours of the rainbow. Par-snails only appear when there is a rainbow in the sky or a witch is having a party. He is a friendly snail who likes you to pick him up and talk to him. He is happy to sit in your hand or on your head!

Par-snails love music and party games. When you play pass the par-snail and the music stops they come out of their shells and wiggle their horns at you. If they sing to you, you have won the game and you get a big chocolate snail. Everyone wins a prize in this game. We are all given a bag of sweetie snails (with heads and tails) a party hat and Harry Potter chocolate frogs!!!

I can't wait for auntie's birthday party! I'm going to give her a black tee-shirt with pink bats flying all over it. I've got sparkly wrapping paper and spellotape. I'm going to draw dragons and pentacles on her birthday card, and inside the card I'll write Happy Birthday from Louise, with Love & Best Witches.

The End

Dear Auntie Nettie,   16/10/07

Halloween soon! I can't wait! That's
why I've sent you some pink witch
hair clips for Halloween night — I
have some too! Hope you like them, I
think they're great. I'm being
a witch for Halloween and we're
having a Halloween party at my house.
I have the full witch's kit: A broom,
3 witch's hats, a raggedy dress, a
shiny belt, spider-web tights (which you
gave me), a home-made wand, plus some
luminous nail-polish and black lipstick.
            Love & Best Witches,
                    Louise

Lightning Source UK Ltd.
Milton Keynes UK
UKOW04f2152041013

218524UK00001B/46/P